LET'S TALK ABOUT
BEING HELPFUL

by Joy Berry • Illustrated by Maggie Smith

SCHOLASTIC INC.

New York Toronto London Auckland Sydney
Mexico City New Delhi Hong Kong Buenos Aires

SCHOLASTIC and associated design is a trademark of Scholastic Inc.

ISBN 0-439-34151-5

10 9 8 7 6 5 4 3 2 1   01 02 03 04 05
Printed in the U.S.A.
First printing, December 2001

Hello, my name is Max.

I live with Carlos.

Sometimes Carlos doesn't want to be helpful.

Especially if it means doing something he doesn't want to do.

You might not want to be helpful if it means doing something you don't want to do.

You might not want to do something because you think it won't be fun.

You might not want to do something because you think it will take too much time or effort.

You might not want to do something
because you would rather do something else.

You might not want to do something
because you want someone else to do it.

If you did only the things you like to do, some important tasks wouldn't get done.

Sometimes you need to be helpful by doing tasks you don't want to do.

Sometimes trying to get out of doing an unwanted task takes more time and effort than doing the task.

Whenever necessary, it's best to do an unwanted task rather than spend time and effort avoiding it.

Don't put off doing a task hoping that you won't have to do it at all. It won't go away.

The only way to get rid of a task is to do it. Once it's done, you can do something else.

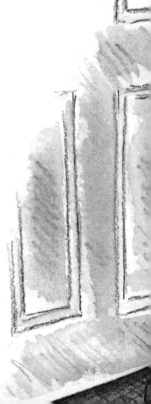

Get unwanted tasks out of the way by doing them immediately.

You'll have more fun doing the things you enjoy if there aren't unwanted tasks waiting for you.

Try not to complain while you are doing an unwanted task.

Complaining will only make a job seem more unpleasant than it actually is.

You might want to play a game with yourself to make your work more fun. Set a time limit for the task. Then try to get the job done in that amount of time.

You might want to offer yourself a reward to motivate yourself to work.

Promise yourself that you'll do something you really want to do after you finish your task. Make sure what you choose to do is okay with your parents or guardians. Then keep your promise.

Try to do every task well so that someone else won't have to do it all over again.

Try to finish your tasks so that they won't have to be finished by another person.

It isn't fair when one person has to do all the tasks that no one else wants to do. When everyone takes turns doing unwanted tasks, it's more fair for everybody. Being helpful by doing your share of the tasks can make everyone happier.

Let's talk about . . . **Joy Berry!**

Joy Berry knows kids. As the inventor of self-help books for kids, she has written over 250 books that teach children about taking responsibility for themselves and their actions. With sales of over 80 million copies, Joy's books have helped millions of parents and their kids.

Through interesting stories that kids can relate to, Joy Berry's *Let's Talk About* books explain how to handle even the toughest situations and emotions. Written in a clear, simple style and illustrated with bright, humorous pictures, the *Let's Talk About* books are fun, informative, and they really work!